Toot & Puddle

by

Holly Hobbie

LITTLE, BROWN AND COMPANY
New York • Boston

Little, Brown and Company

Hachette Book Group
237 Park Avenue, New York, NY 10017
Visit our website at www.lb-kids.com

Little, Brown and Company is a division of Hachette Book Group, Inc.
The Little, Brown name and logo are trademarks of Hachette Book Group, Inc.

First Paperback Edition: September 2010

First published in hardcover in September 1997 by Little, Brown and Company

Library of Congress Cataloging-in-Publication Data

Hobbie, Holly.
Toot and Puddle / by Holly Hobbie. — 1st ed.
p. cm.
Summary: Toot and Puddle are best friends with very different interests, so when
Toot spends the year traveling around the world, Puddle enjoys receiving his postcards.
ISBN 0-316-36552-1 (hc)
ISBN 0-316-16702-9 (Anniversary) / 978-0-316-08080-4 (pb)
[1. Pigs — Fiction. 2. Travel — Fiction. 3. Friendship — Fiction.
4. Postcards — Fiction. I. Title.
PZ7.H6515Ad 1997
[E] — dc20   96-28649

10 9 8 7 6 5 4 3 2 1

SC

Printed in China

The paintings for this book were done in watercolor.
The text was set in Optima, and the display type is Windsor Light.

Toot and Puddle lived together in Woodcock Pocket.

It was such a perfect place to be that Puddle never wanted to go anywhere else.

Toot, on the other hand, loved to take trips. He had been to Cape Cod, the Grand Canyon, and the redwood forests.

One day in January, Toot decided to set off on his biggest trip ever.
He decided to see the world. "Do you want to come along?" he asked
Puddle. "We could start with someplace warm and wild."

 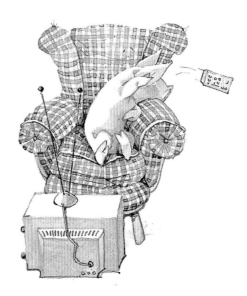 

Puddle preferred to stay home.

I love snow, he thought.

Dear Puddle,
I've made some
new friends in
Africa! Is winter
getting boring?

Toot

To: Puddle
Woodcock Pocket
U.S.A.

PAR AVION

FEBRUARY
KENYA AFRICA
AM
1997

Meanwhile…presenting Puddle at Pocket Pond!

MARCH ON THE NILE

Dear Puddle,
  EGYPT is awesome.
The Pyramids are
the greatest. Wish
you COULD MEET me
  at the Oasis.
    Your Friend,
      TooT

To: Puddle
  WOODCOCK POCKET
      U.S.A.

PAR AVION

March meant maple syrup. Puddle wished Toot were there to taste the pancakes.

Yes, spring had arrived. Puddle was having mud season. Yay!

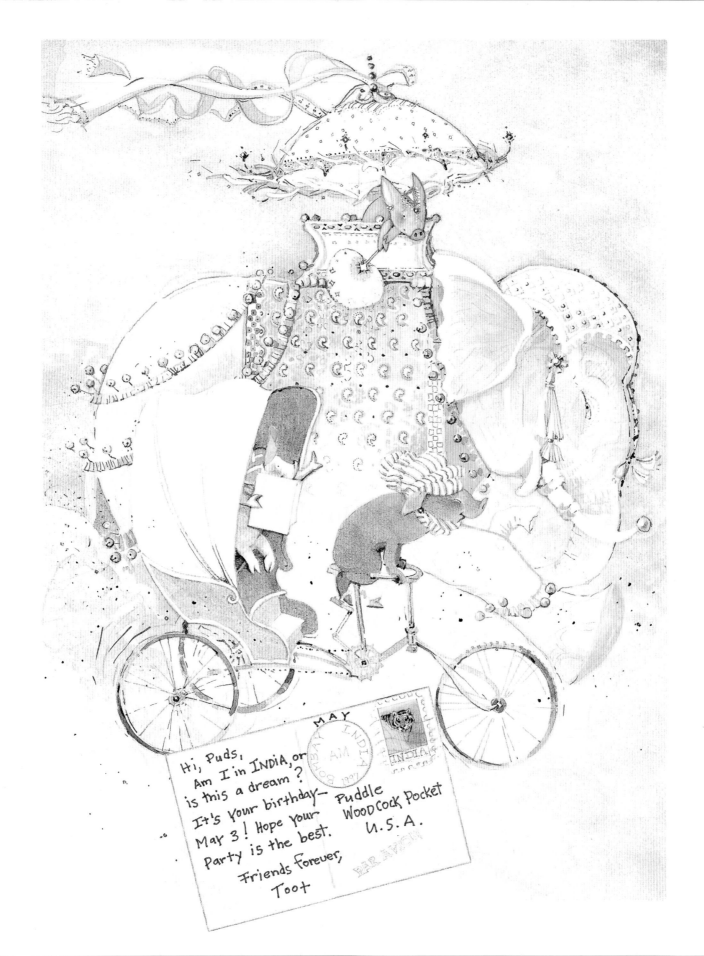

Back at Woodcock Pocket…
"For he's a jolly good fellow,
 for he's a jolly good fellow,
 for he's a jolly good fellow,
 that nobody can deny!"

Puddle remembered.

In July…presenting Puddle at Pocket Pond! Every time he jumped in, he cheered, *"Olé!"*

Dear Puddle,
   August is cold in
Antarctica, but I've
made more friends
here than anywhere
yet. Are you going
to the beach this
year? I miss you.
Do you miss me?
      Friends Forever,
         Toot

To: Puddle
Woodcock Pocket
U.S.A.

Yes, Puddle missed his friend.

Dear Pudsy,
Bonjour from Paris!
   Art is everywhere!
Love is in the air!
   Au revoir,
      Toot

To:
Puddle
Woodcock Pocket
   U.S.A.

I love art, thought Puddle.

Dearest Pudsio,
Italy is heaven—
it's one big treat!

Your Friend,

Tootsio

To:
Puddle
Woodcock Pocket
U. S. A.

ITALY

OCTOBER
AM
FLORENCE ITALY

VIA AEREA

Meanwhile, it was Halloween in Woodcock Pocket.

Puddle decided to be horrifying.

One morning in November, Toot woke up and thought, *It's time to go home.*

Yay, Toot's coming!

December called for celebration.
"Here's to all your adventures
around the world," said Puddle.
"Here's to all your adventures
right at home," said Toot.

"And here's to being together
again," Toot and Puddle
said at the same time.

Toot was happy to be back in his own bed, and Puddle was happy, too.

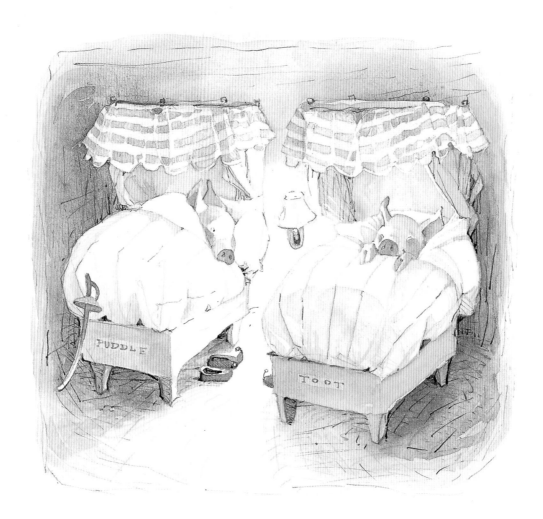

"I wonder if it will snow all night," Puddle said.
"I hope so," said Toot.
"Then we'll go sliding," said Puddle.
"And skiing," said Toot.
"Good night, Toot."
"Good night, Puddle."